This dragon book belongs to:

....

Teach Your Dragon to Stop Lying
My Dragon Books - Volume 15
Written by Steve Herman

ISBN: 978-1948040419 (paperback)
ISBN: 978-1948040426 (hardcover)

www.MyDragonBooks.com

First Edition: July 2018

10 9 8 7 6 5 4 3 2 1

Don't be afraid or run away –
My Diggory Doo is tamed!
Though dragons can be scary,
not all dragons are the same.

One time Diggory said, "I'm done!"
but what he'd done instead –
Was stuffing his dirty clothes
and toys underneath his bed!

Mother baked a chocolate pie
but said we had to wait –
"You can have a slice," she said,
"when you have cleaned your plate."

Diggory caught a little fish,
but told a whopping tale
That with nothing but a fishing pole,
he had caught a WHALE!

"Diggory Doo," I told him,
"it should come as no surprise
If your teacher gets suspicious
that you might be telling lies."

"No throwing balls inside the house,"
Mom warned us everyday,
But Diggory disobeyed mom
and did it anyway.

When mom heard the mirror break,
she ran to see –
"It was Drew," said Diggory Doo.
"I swear it wasn't me!"

"This has got to stop," I cried.
(I was really getting mad),
But Diggory did not understand
why telling lies was bad.

"You can't be truly happy
when you know you're being bad;
When you have a guilty heart,
it leads to feeling sad."

"When you do what you should not,
be honest and admit it;
Don't put the blame on someone else
when you're the one who did it."

Diggory looked a little shocked and said, "I never knew That so much damage could be done by telling what's not true!"

I DON'T BELIEVE YOU

Get your FREE Gift from Diggory Doo at
www.MyDragonBooks.com/gift

Read more about Drew and Diggory Doo!

Visit
www.MyDragonBooks.com
for more!

图书在版编目(CIP)数据

狼和七只小羊/红马文化编.—北京:知识出版社,
2008.5
(我最喜欢的经典童话故事精绘本)
ISBN 978-7-5015-5512-3

Ⅰ.狼… Ⅱ.红… Ⅲ.汉语拼音—儿童读物 Ⅳ.H125.4

中国版本图书馆 CIP 数据核字(2008)第 062349 号

狼和七只小羊

策　　　划	刘东风　　刘庆源	
编　　　著	红马文化　RED HORSE	
文 字 改 编	张　文	
美 术 统 筹	庄健宇	
绘　　　画	王　洋	
版 面 设 计	赵　曦	
作 者 统 筹	张洪霞	
责 任 编 辑	李　文　　梁嫱曦	
责 任 印 制	乌　灵	
出 版 发 行	知识出版社	
社　　　址	北京阜成门北大街 17 号	
邮　　　编	100037	
电　　　话	010-88390732	
网　　　址	www.ecph.com.cn	
经　　　销	新华书店	
印　　　刷	北京地大彩印厂	
开　　　本	889 × 1194　1/16	
印　　　张	1.5 印张	
版　　　次	2008 年 5 月第 1 版	
印　　　次	2008 年 5 月第 1 次印刷	
印　　　数	1~15000	
定　　　价	10.00 元	

狼和七只小羊

LANG HE QIZHI XIAOYANG

〔德〕 格林兄弟

知藏出版社

从前，森林里住着山羊妈妈和她的七个孩子。小山羊们又聪明又活泼，山羊妈妈可喜欢他们啦。

一天，山羊妈妈要去找吃的了。出门前，她对孩子们说："你们乖乖在家呆着，谁来也别开门。特别是老狼，如果让他进屋，他会把你们全都吃掉的。老狼常把自己化装成别的样子，不过，你们只要一听到他粗哑的声音，一看到他黑黑的爪子，就能认出他来啦。"

小山羊们说："放心吧，妈妈，我们会当心的。"

méi guò duō jiǔ　　lǎo láng jiù lái qiāo mén le　　tā zhàn zài mén wài dà shēng shuō
没过多久，老狼就来敲门了。他站在门外大声说：
hái zi men kāi mén a　　mā ma huí lái la　　mā ma dài huí le xiān nèn de qīng
"孩子们，开门啊，妈妈回来啦！妈妈带回了鲜嫩的青
cǎo　　nǐ men bù xiǎng cháng cháng ma
草，你们不想尝尝吗？"

xiǎo shān yáng men tīng dào lǎo láng de shēng yīn　　lì kè jiào qǐ lái　　mā ma
小山羊们听到老狼的声音，立刻叫起来："妈妈
de shēng yīn yòu xì yòu hǎo tīng　　nǐ de shēng yīn yòu cū yòu yǎ　　nǐ bú shì wǒ men
的声音又细又好听，你的声音又粗又哑！你不是我们
de mā ma　　nǐ shì lǎo láng
的妈妈，你是老狼！"

老狼跑到杂货店，买了一大块白垩土吃下了肚，声音马上就变细了。他又回来敲山羊家的门，用细细的声音喊道："孩子们，开门啊，妈妈回来啦！妈妈带回了新鲜的水果，你们不想尝尝吗？"

小山羊们看到老狼搭在窗户上的黑爪子，立刻叫起来："妈妈没有这样的黑爪子！你不是我们的妈妈，你是老狼！"

老狼跑到面包师那里，说：
"我的脚受伤了，给我用面团儿揉揉吧。"等面包师给他揉过之后，他去找磨坊主，说："在我的脚上洒点儿面粉吧。"

磨坊主说："我才不干这种事，免得你又去骗人。"

"不肯？那我就把你吃掉！"

磨坊主害怕了，只好洒了点儿面粉，把老狼的爪子弄成了白色。

老狼又跑到山羊家，一边敲门一边说："孩子们，开门啊，妈妈回来啦！"

小山羊们喊："抬起你的爪子给我们看看吧！"

老狼把爪子伸进窗户，小山羊们看到爪子是白色的，便相信了他的话，把门打开了。

老狼闯进屋，小山羊们吓得东躲西藏。第一只小山羊跑到了桌子底下，第二只钻到了被子里，第三只躲到了炉子里，第四只跑进了厨房，第五只藏进了柜子，第六只蹲在洗脸盆底下，第七只藏到了钟盒里。老狼把他们一只一只找出来吞下了肚，只有躲在钟盒里的那只最小的山羊没被发现。

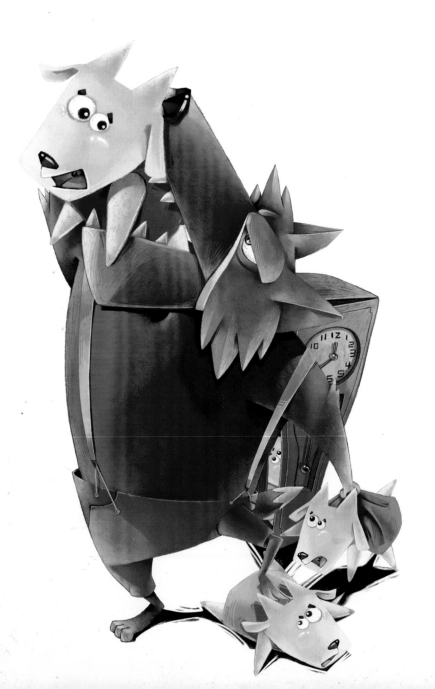

老狼一连吞下六只小山羊，肚子撑得圆鼓鼓的。

这下，他心满意足了，踱着方步走出山羊的家。

前面的草地上有棵大树。老狼走到树底下，躺下来呼呼大睡。

shān yáng mā ma huí lái le　ā　zhè shì zěn me huí shì　wū mén chǎng kāi
山羊妈妈回来了。啊,这是怎么回事?屋门敞开

zhe zhuō zi hé yǐ zi dōng dǎo xī wāi　xǐ liǎn pén shuāi chéng le suì piàn er　bèi
着,桌子和椅子东倒西歪,洗脸盆摔成了碎片儿,被

zi hé zhěn tou diào dào le dì shang　ér tā de hái zi men yí gè dōu bú jiàn le
子和枕头掉到了地上,而她的孩子们一个都不见了。

tā jiào zhe hái zi men de míng zi　kě shì méi yǒu yí gè dā ying　zuì hòu
她叫着孩子们的名字,可是没有一个答应。最后,

dāng tā jiào dào zuì xiǎo de shān yáng shí　yí gè shēng yīn cóng zhōng hé li xiǎng qǐ
当她叫到最小的山羊时,一个声音从钟盒里响起

lái　mā ma　wǒ zài zhè er ne
来:"妈妈,我在这儿呢!"

xiǎo shān yáng gào su mā ma lǎo láng bǎ gē ge jiě jie dōu chī diào le　shān yáng
小山羊告诉妈妈老狼把哥哥姐姐都吃掉了。山羊

mā ma tīng le　kū de bié tí duō shāng xīn la
妈妈听了,哭得别提多伤心啦。

shān yáng mā ma hé xiǎo shān yáng zǒu chū qù　　fā xiàn lǎo láng tǎng zài dà shù dǐ
山羊妈妈和小山羊走出去，发现老狼躺在大树底

xia shuì de zhèng xiāng ne　　tā de dù zi gǔ de lǎo gāo　　lǐ miàn yǒu shén me dōng xi
下睡得正香呢。他的肚子鼓得老高，里面有什么东西

dòng gè bù tíng
动个不停。

tiān na　　　　shān yáng mā ma shuō　　nán dào bèi tā tūn xià qù de hái zi
"天哪，"山羊妈妈说，"难道被他吞下去的孩子

men hái huó zhe ma
们还活着吗？"

xiǎo shān yáng pǎo huí jiā　　ná lái jiǎn dāo hé zhēn xiàn　　shān yáng mā ma jiǎn kāi
小山羊跑回家，拿来剪刀和针线。山羊妈妈剪开

lǎo láng de dù zi　　liù zhī xiǎo shān yáng yì zhī jiē yì zhī tiào le chū lái　　yì diǎn
老狼的肚子，六只小山羊一只接一只跳了出来，一点

er dōu méi shòu shāng　　shān yáng mā ma gāo xìng de bào zhe hái zi men yòu bèng yòu tiào
儿都没受伤。山羊妈妈高兴地抱着孩子们又蹦又跳。

山羊妈妈说："老狼太可恶了，我们得惩罚他一下。你们去找些大石头来，趁他没醒，把石头装到他的肚子里去。"

七只小山羊飞快地拖来很多石头，拼命往老狼肚子里塞。石头塞满后，山羊妈妈把他的肚皮缝了起来。老狼打着呼噜，一点儿都没发觉。

过了一会儿，老狼醒了。他觉得口渴，想到井边去喝水，可是每走一步，肚子里就发出哗啦哗啦的响声。他还不知道自己的肚子里被装满了石头呢！

到了井边,老狼弯腰去喝水,可肚子里的石头太沉了,一下子把他带到了井里面。老狼掉进井里淹死了,七只小山羊高兴地叫道:"老狼死了!老狼死了!"他们和妈妈一起围着水井跳起舞来。没有了老狼的威胁,从此,他们过着无忧无虑的日子,真是快乐极了。